The Prin
and the Dr

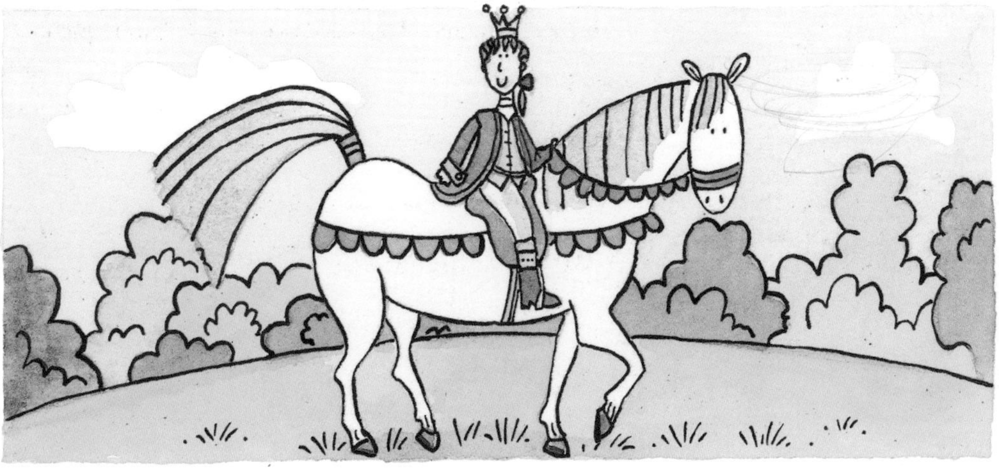

Monica Hughes
Illustrated by Lucy Grossmith

RIGBY

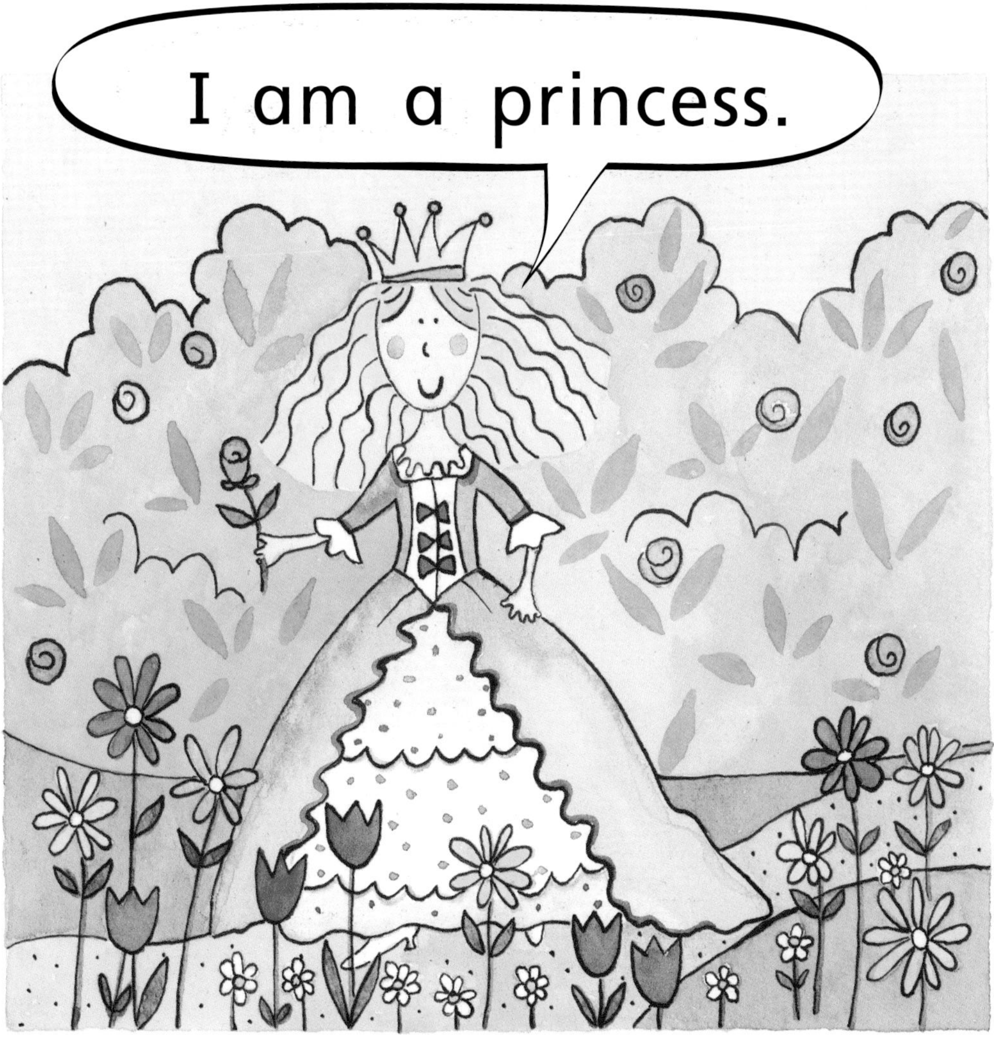
I am a princess.

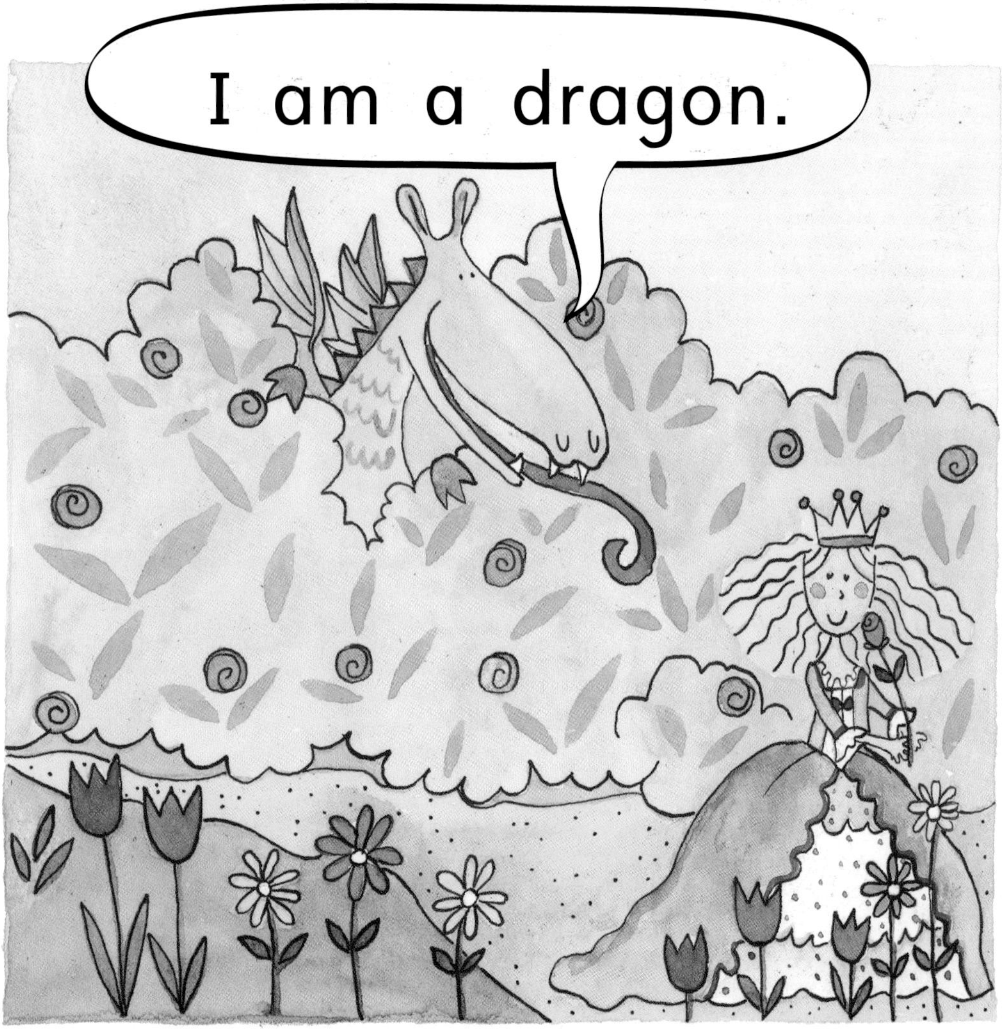
I am a dragon.

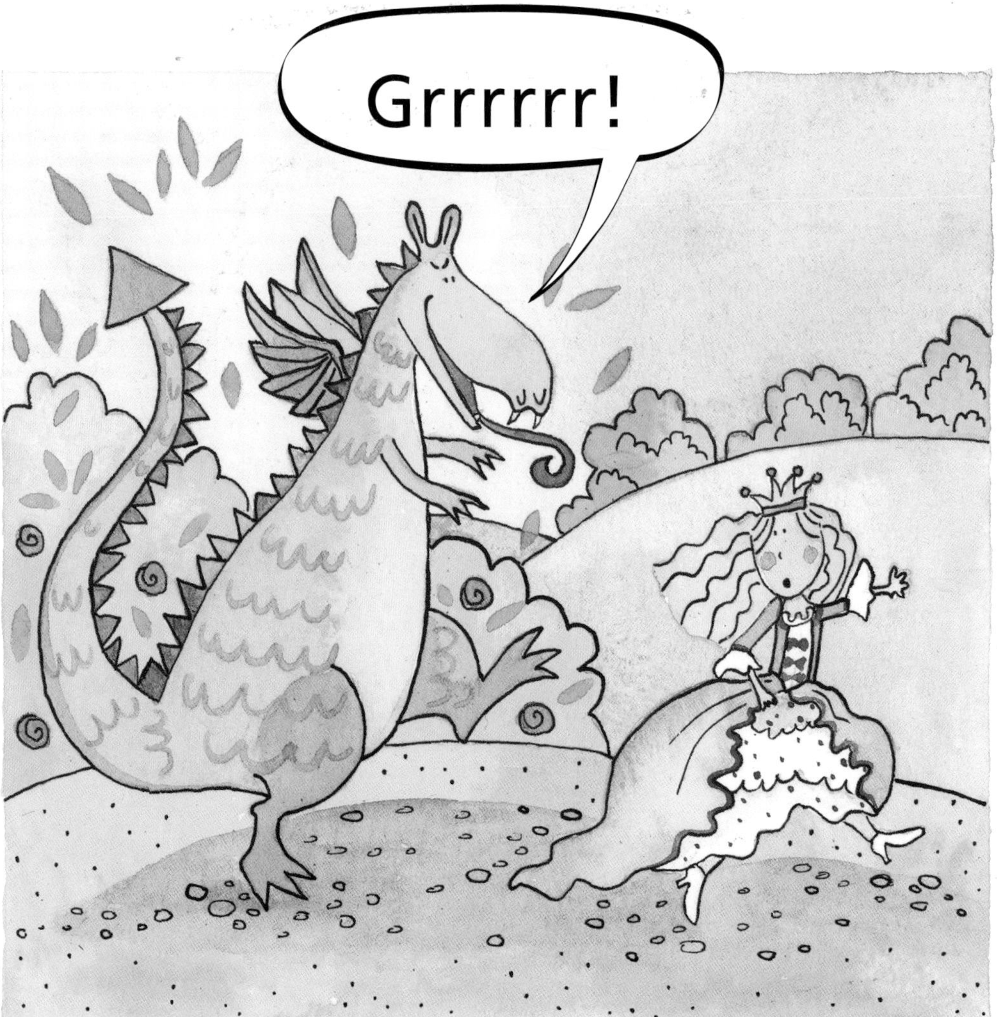
Grrrrrr!

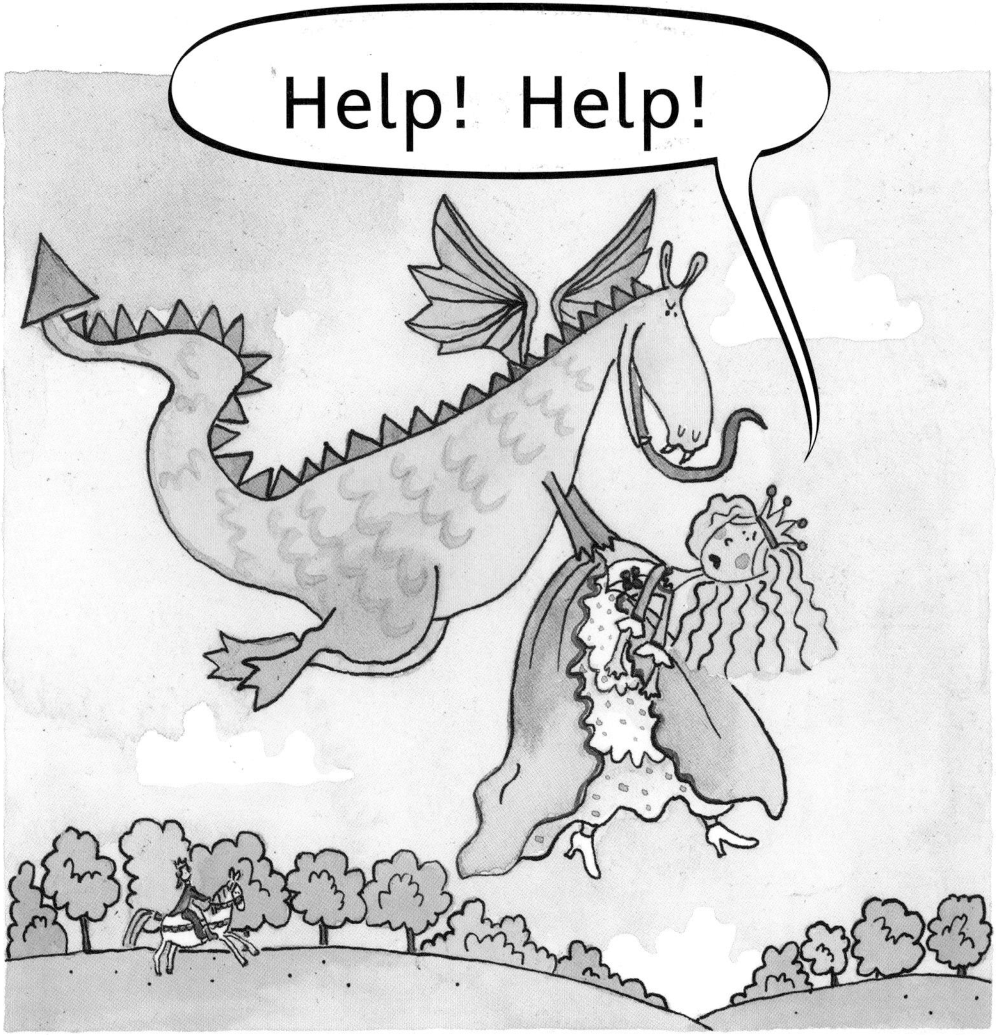
Help! Help!

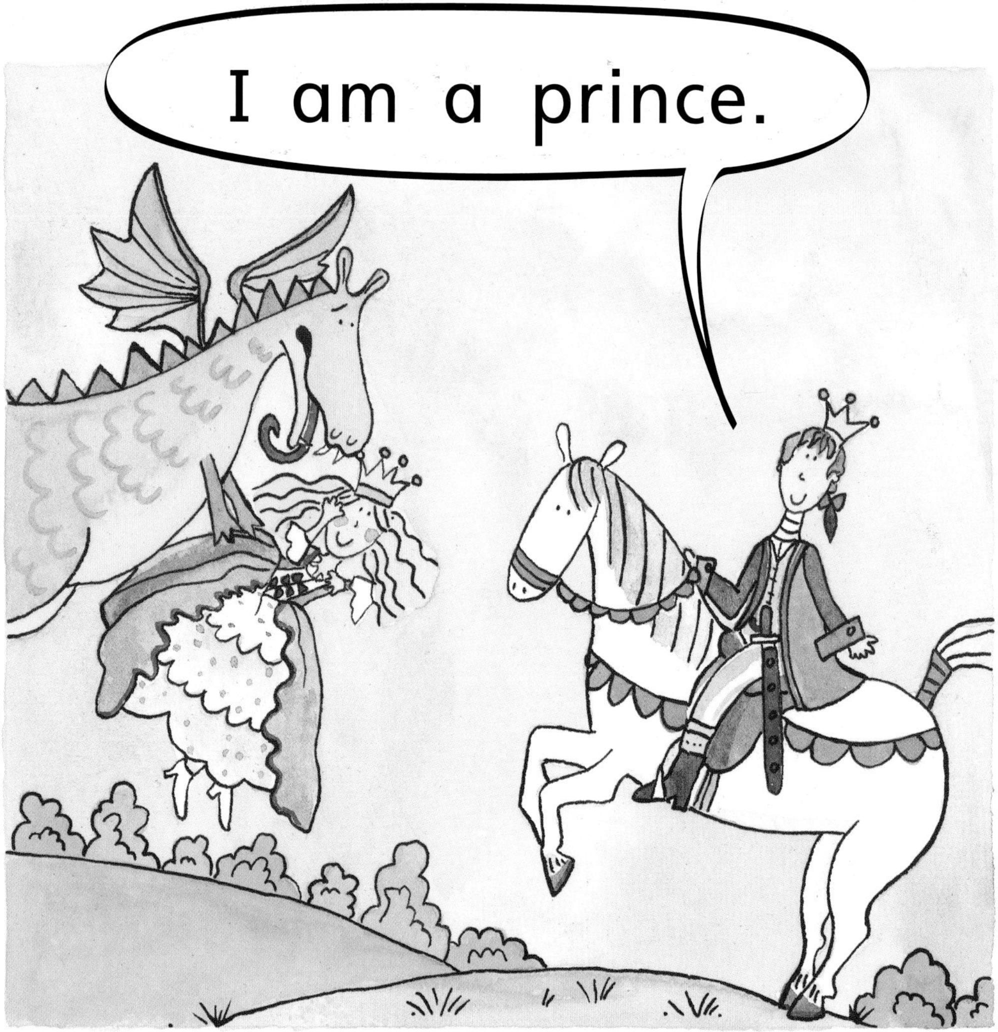
I am a prince.

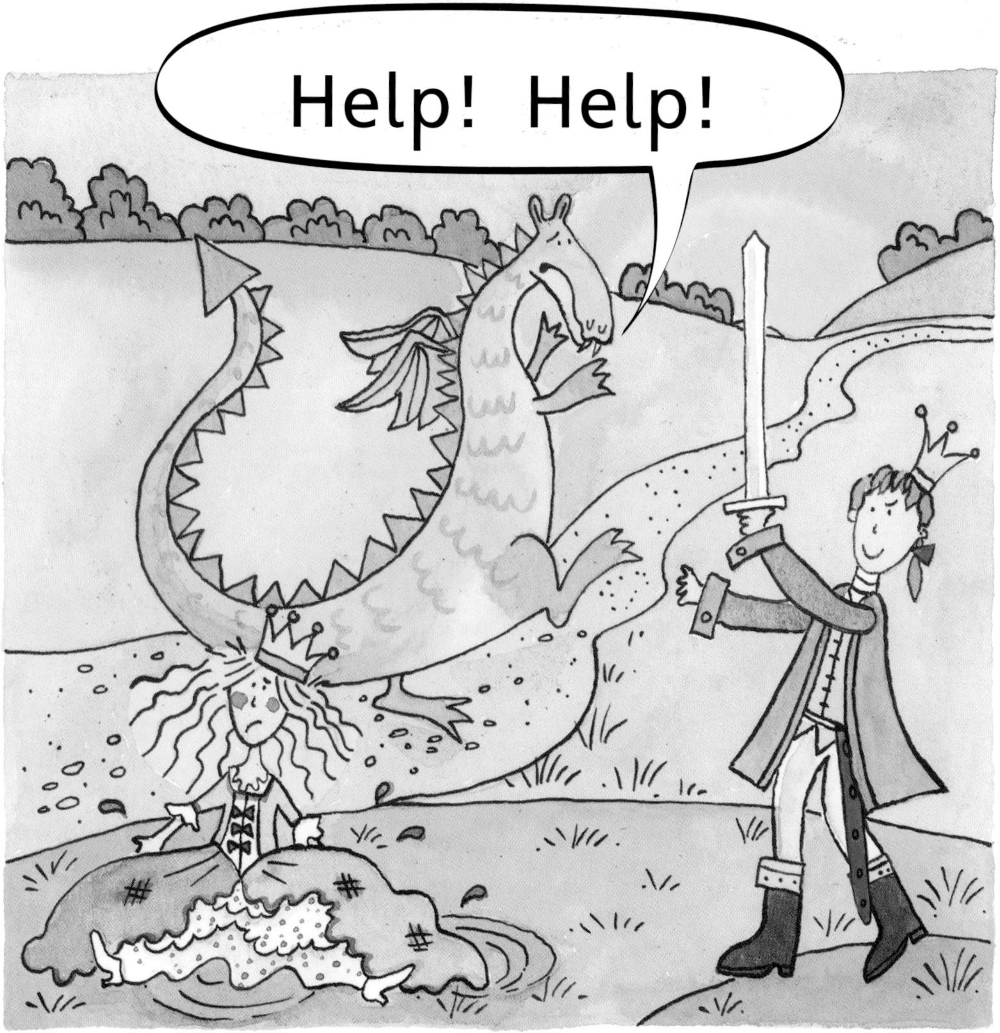
Help! Help!

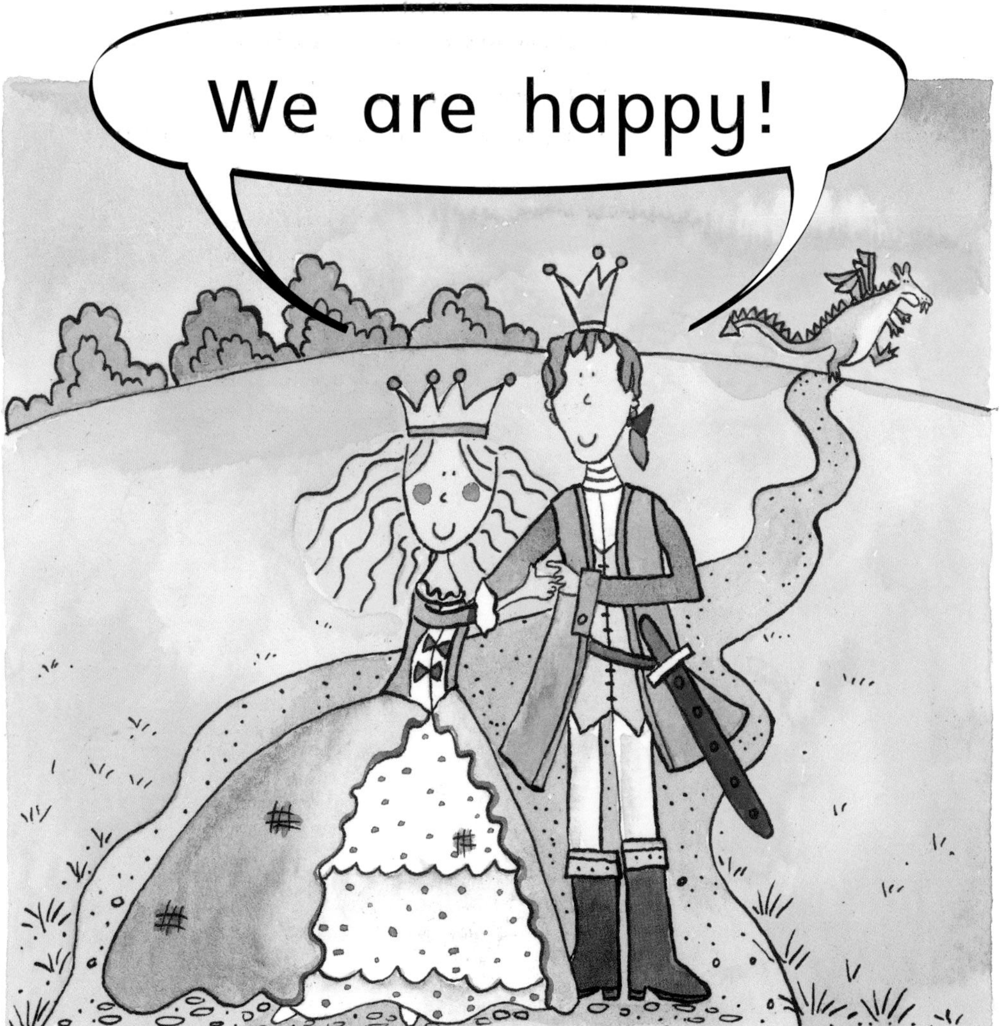
We are happy!